The Alden Family Mysteries
by Gertrude Chandler Warner

GERTRUDE CHANDLER WARNER

SNOWBOUND MYSTERY

Illustrated by David Cunningham

ALBERT WHITMAN & Com~~~~~~~~~ es, Illinois

ISBN 0-8075-7517-8
L.C. Catalog Card 68-9124
Copyright © 1968 by Albert Whitman & Company
Published simultaneously in Canada by General Publishing, Limited, Toronto.
Printed in the United States of America.
12   11   10

Contents

CHAPTER 1

Trip—or Adventure?

It was a lovely autumn day. The sun was warm and the sky was blue. The Alden family sat around the breakfast table, talking as usual. First they talked about the Greenfield schools being closed for a week. There had been a fire. Some of the schoolrooms had to be painted and repaired.

"You know what I want to do?" Benny Alden asked suddenly.

"No, what?" asked his big brother Henry. He smiled because Benny was always wanting to do funny things.

Grandfather Alden laughed, too. He said, "Tell us, Ben. I am always interested in anything you want to do."

Benny put down his spoon. He had just finished an enormous dish of cereal and milk.

"Well," he said, "I'd like to go up to the Oak Hill woods and live in that hunters' cabin. Henry still has a week before he has to go back to college. We could all go."

Grandfather Alden said, "I think it could be managed. I belong to the Sportsmen's Club that owns the cabin. The hunters don't use it at this time of the year." He set down his coffee cup. "The cabin isn't too far away, and it's too early for snow."

"That's exactly what I thought," said Benny. "It's much too early for snow. We could do a lot of hiking in the fall woods. We might see wild animals like deer and find new plants."

"What about food?" asked Henry. "You'll be the first one to be hungry, Ben."

"Oh, that will be part of the fun!" said Benny. "I talked with Mr. Robbins. He's one of Grandfather's friends who belongs to the Sportsmen's Club, too."

"And what did he tell you?" asked Grandfather.

"We can hike five miles a day to the little store on the other side of Oak Hill. There's a good path and we can't miss the way. We can buy what we need at Nelson's Store."

"I see you've got it all figured out," said Henry. "Two and a half miles each way. Can we cook in the cabin, Grandfather?"

"Well, yes. There's a cookstove that burns kerosene. You could certainly heat up baked beans."

"And water," added Violet.

"Well, a panful maybe," replied Grandfather, laughing. "But not too many baths."

"That suits me," said Benny.

"Well, it wouldn't suit me," said Mr. Alden. "I think I'll stay at home."

"We'd love to have you come along, Grandfather," said Violet. "Don't you really want to go?"

"No, my dear. I really want to stay at home. I'll go with you as far as Henry can drive the car, and then I'll take the car back home. I'll meet you in about a week. We can plan that."

Henry said, "Benny, suppose we run out of

food and don't feel like walking five miles to the store?"

"Well, we could always walk home," said Benny, but he was joking. "I'll take my transistor radio so we can hear all the news."

"I'd love to go," Jessie said. "We've never had an adventure in cold weather before."

"Why do you call it an adventure, Jessie?" asked Benny. "It's just a trip."

"All right, then," agreed Jessie. "But you know that our trips always turn out to be adventures. We might as well expect something surprising. We can take Watch this time. He will be glad. This is just the kind of trip for him."

Watch was the Aldens' dog. He seemed to understand everything that Jessie said. Now he knew that the Aldens were talking about him. He wagged his short tail because Jessie had said, "We'll take Watch."

"He knows he's going this time," said Henry, looking at the big dog.

"Yes, he's laughing," said Benny. "Look."

Watch seemed to be saying, "I'm ready. Let's go."

The Alden family started out for the Oak Hill woods on a beautiful day. The sun shone on the bright red and yellow leaves of the maple trees, and the sky was very blue.

Each of the Aldens took a sleeping bag. They all wore heavy clothes and took a few extra ones for cold nights.

Henry drove the car as far as he could. He stopped where a path led up a thickly wooded hill.

Jessie, Violet, Henry, and Benny got out. So did Watch. The Aldens took their sleeping bags, knapsacks, and the food.

Watch began to bark and jump. He knew something different was going to happen.

"You think you're a puppy again, Watch," said Jessie, laughing. "Don't you know you're getting to be an old dog?"

No, Watch didn't know that. He felt like a puppy—he was so glad to be walking in the woods with his family.

When the young people said good-bye to Mr. Alden, Watch put his front paws on the door of the car and barked good-bye, too. Mr. Alden patted his head and said, "I'll miss you, Watch. Remember, I'll meet all of you here one week from today at ten o'clock in the morning."

The Aldens waved until the car was out of sight. Then the climb began. There was a foot-path, but it was narrow. They walked in line, Benny leading the way.

The woods smelled of evergreens and pine needles. Yellow and red leaves floated down all along the way.

"I can hardly wait to get there," Benny said.

Henry laughed. "Just keep on walking, Ben," he said.

CHAPTER 2

Cabin in the Woods

Long before the family saw the cabin, Watch began to bark. His bark sounded different to the Aldens. They all looked ahead. There stood the little log cabin. They walked up to it as fast as they could. The door was locked, but Henry had the key.

Watch was the first one inside. He ran around with his nose to the floor, smelling everything. The Aldens came in after Watch. They found themselves in one room with a bare table and six plain chairs at one end. Under the one window by the table was a long window seat with hard, brown cushions on it.

When Benny saw the window seat, he said, "That makes me think of the night we spent in the baker's shop before we found the boxcar. I think I'll sleep there just for fun."

Henry said, "I think it will only be one night, Ben. Those cushions look hard."

Jessie said, "I like the couch better." She poked the bright green couch as she spoke. "Oh, this is old, but it's soft! I guess it's for company. It opens out into a double bed."

"Well, we don't need it," said Henry. "We certainly won't have company."

"We can sit on it," said Benny. "And look at Watch! He can lie on it."

Jessie looked at Watch and laughed. The dog already lay stretched out on the couch.

"You think I'm going to make you get off," Jessie said. "But you can stay this time, Watch. You can't hurt that old couch."

At the other end of the room was an oilstove. Beside it was a small sink with one faucet.

"Cold," said Benny, trying it.

"Of course, Ben," said Henry. "What did you expect? Hot water? That's spring water."

There were two shelves and a drawer beside the sink. On the shelf were a few dishes. A neat pile of firewood was stacked against the wall.

"Oh, we have a fireplace," said Violet. "How nice. That's what the wood is for."

Just over the fireplace was a shelf with two lanterns and two candles on it. Beside the fireplace were two long-handled shovels and an ax.

There were two small bedrooms at the left side of the front door. Jessie lifted the curtain over the door to one bedroom and saw two bunk beds. The other room was the same.

Without a word, the Aldens put their sleeping bags on the four bunks. They set their knapsacks down and went back to the living room. On the table was a thick, black book.

"Oh, yes!" exclaimed Henry. "This must be the Visitors' Book. Remember, Grandfather told us to be sure to write our names and the date in this book. Here's an empty page."

Henry took out a pen and wrote his name and address and the date. Then he gave the pen to Jessie. Each one wrote his name on the page.

After that, Violet turned back to read the first

pages of the book. There were many rows of names.

"Here's the storeman's name, Thomas Nelson!" cried Benny. "Why should he come up here?"

"Maybe he comes to hunt," answered Henry.

"But he lives in the woods now," said Benny. "He wouldn't have to come to the cabin to hunt."

Henry said, "It is strange, Benny, that he should bring his family. I guess this must be his wife, Barbara Nelson. And here's Puggsy Nelson. That must be a little boy."

"Maybe it's a little girl," said Jessie.

"I don't think it could be a girl," said Henry. "They wouldn't call a girl Puggsy even as a nickname. But why should he bring his family with him, anyway?"

"Oh, let's sit on the window seat and look through this book," said Jessie, taking off her thick jacket. "I'd like to see who else we'll find. We've got lots of time."

They took off their coats and all four sat down on the window seat. Henry turned the pages as they read off the names.

"Here's Mr. Robert Robbins. He's one of Grandfather's friends," Henry said. He turned another page.

"Oh, look! Here's the Nelson family again!" said Benny.

"Now, why do you suppose they came twice?" asked Violet. "It couldn't be to hunt."

"Ah," said Benny, trying to be funny. "A mystery! Jessie said we always have a mystery."

"No, Ben," Jessie laughed. "I didn't say a mystery. I said an adventure."

"Well, you were right, weren't you?" asked Benny. "Isn't this an adventure?"

Henry said, "I'd call this a mystery, myself. Look." He pointed to an earlier page. There was the Nelson family a third time.

"Now, everyone listen," said Jessie. "We don't need any groceries. But let's go down to Nelson's Store and just look around. What do you say?"

"Good," said Violet and Henry together.

Benny said, "I agree, but wouldn't it be a good idea to eat lunch first?"

Henry shut the book and got up. "I told you, Ben, you'd be the first to be hungry. But I don't blame you. I'm hungry myself after that climb. When's lunch?"

Jessie and Violet were already in the kitchen, which was only the other end of the room.

"Let's have sandwiches," said Benny. "They don't take long. For supper we can cook things and have a fire in the fireplace."

"A good idea," said Violet. "I'd like a tuna fish sandwich. I hope we brought a can opener."

"We did," said Jessie. "And if we didn't, remember Benny has his pocketknife."

Benny's pocketknife had everything in it, from a screwdriver to a small pair of scissors.

Violet hunted in the kitchen drawer and found a red-and-white plastic tablecloth. She spread this on the table. Then Violet ran outside and soon came back with some red and yellow leaves. She put these in a small white bowl in the middle of the table.

"I could eat ten sandwiches, Jessie," said Benny.

"All right. Wait till you eat two, and then I'll

make more. But I'll have to open another can of tuna fish."

When the sandwiches were gone, along with many cups of milk, Benny found that he didn't want any more after all. They ate bananas for dessert.

As they sat there eating, Jessie said, "Let's unpack everything before we go and see if we want to take anything with us on the hike."

"Let's take the field glasses," said Benny. "In case we see any birds."

Violet said, "Shh, look! Look out into the tree."

There was a woodpecker on the trunk, and a goldfinch and a chickadee flying among the branches.

Jessie said, "It's a good thing we saw the birds before we went. We can buy some sunflower seed and set up a bird feeder."

"While we're at the store," said Benny, "maybe we can find out if Puggsy is a name for a boy or a girl."

"Do you know the way, Benny?" asked Violet.

"No, but I guess I can find it. There is only one path."

"Grandfather said he was sure we couldn't miss it," Violet said.

"And lock the door!" sang Benny. He and Watch were already chasing each other.

Down the path they went, looking on every side for something new. A rabbit scuttled away far ahead of them, showing his short white tail.

"Look!" said Violet. "He's scared. Maybe he never saw people before."

Just then Watch smelled the rabbit. He started to run so suddenly he almost turned head over heels.

"Watch!" called Henry. "Stop that!"

But Watch wouldn't mind Henry or anyone else—except Jessie.

She called, "Watch, stop this minute!"

Poor Watch stopped so fast he skidded on his side. He always obeyed Jessie. He looked up at her now with sad eyes.

"I'm sorry, Watch. Yes, I know," said Jessie, patting his head, "it's too bad. But you can't kill rabbits, that's sure. Understand?"

Watch was sorry, but he seemed to understand. He trotted along with the family.

Then Violet found some trailing vines and red berries. "On the way back, I'll pick them. Then we'll have something pretty to look at in our cabin," she said.

But Henry was not looking at the ground. He was looking up into the trees. In fact, he stopped for a minute to look up.

"What are you looking for?" asked Benny.

"I'm not looking for anything," Henry answered. "But these trees are nut trees. It's possible we could find some hickory nuts still on the ground. I see a few left in the trees."

"Oh," said Jessie. "Those nuts are delicious. We could get a lot and crack them at the cabin."

"It's a lot of fun to find them," said Violet. "But don't you think we had better go nutting another day? We still have to find Nelson's Store."

"Yes, that's so," replied Jessie.

"We want to get home before dark," Henry said. "Remember, we don't know much about this country."

CHAPTER 3

Noises in the Night

At last the Aldens saw the store. There were a few small houses on the other side of the store.

Jessie looked down the road. She said, "This looks like a small village."

Benny read the sign:

NELSON'S STORE

He said, "I think the Nelsons must live upstairs over the store."

"I think so, too," said Jessie. "See the white curtains?"

"I suppose people shop here who live nearby and don't want to drive into Greenfield," Henry said.

The Aldens went in. When they opened the door, a bell rang. But the storeman did not need the bell to tell him someone was coming. He was right behind the counter.

The Aldens didn't know what they had expected to see. But the Nelson family certainly surprised them.

Mr. Nelson was young, for one thing. Henry thought he looked almost as if he were still in college. He was handsome, with brown hair and brown eyes. Although he was tall and slender, he looked strong. Best of all was his smile.

"I'm glad to see visitors," he said to the Aldens. "I'm Tom Nelson. It gets lonesome here when summer is over. Not many customers."

"Our name is Alden," said Henry.

"Oh, yes, I heard you were coming. I have met your grandfather," the young man said. "He's a fine gentleman."

"Yes, he is," said Benny. "I'm Benny, and this is Watch. Do you allow dogs in your store?"

"It all depends on the dog," said Mr. Nelson, laughing. "Your dog seems to have good manners."

Watch was sitting down just inside the door, because Jessie had trained him that way. Once in a while he wiggled his nose and sniffed because a wonderful smell of baking filled the air.

"We are living in the hunters' cabin," said Jessie.

"Fine," said the man. "I'll be glad to help you out in any way I can."

Just then a nice looking young woman with a little boy of about five appeared from behind a curtain.

"Puggsy!" cried Benny.

"How'd you know my name?" asked Puggsy, going right over to Benny. "I don't know you."

"We saw your name in the Visitors' Book in the cabin," explained Jessie. Then she was surprised to see Mrs. Nelson turn red and look at her husband.

The young man said, "Yes, we go up there once in a while. It's a change and very quiet."

"I should think you'd go to town instead," said Benny, "if you want a change. The cabin is even lonesomer than the store."

The young man didn't seem to know what to

say to this. He stood on one foot and then on the other. Then he turned around and took down a jar of pickles, and then he put it back on the shelf.

"We'd like to buy those pickles," said Jessie. "We all like sweet pickles and we didn't bring any."

Puggsy reached up and took hold of Benny's hand. "We look and look at the cabin. We look—"

His mother said, "Puggsy, come here and let me fix your shirt."

Jessie said, as if nothing had happened, "We just used up a can of tuna fish and we ought to get another." She looked at her list.

"Barbara," said Mr. Nelson, "please get the tuna for Miss Alden. It's on your side."

Barbara Nelson seemed glad to do this. As she turned her back, she said, "You people look around the store. You may see something else you need."

"I know what you need," said Puggsy. "You need some buns."

"Oh, yes!" said Mr. Nelson. "Puggsy's right. They are very good. Very good indeed. But—"

"But what?" asked Benny.

"Well, nothing. I just could make them better than I do. My father and grandfather were both bakers. They made the best buns in the world."

"You like to cook, don't you?" asked Jessie. She liked it, too, and she noticed how Mr. Nelson smiled when he talked about it.

Mrs. Nelson answered for him. Mr. Nelson seemed to be dreaming about something. "Yes,

Tom loves to cook. He's a born baker. He is never so happy as when he is making bread, pies, cookies, and cake. Buns are what he most likes to bake."

"I like to bake, too," said Puggsy.

His mother laughed. "Yes, he really does. He can make nice round buns all by himself."

Puggsy took Benny's hand. "I like you, Benny," he said. "You're so nice. You ought to buy some of my mother's beef stew. It goes good with buns."

"Goes *well* with buns, Puggsy," said his mother.

"Well, it means just the same," said Puggsy. "My father's buns have raisins in them. And my mother's stew has onions in it."

"Let's try them both," said Henry. "The stew and the buns. Jessie's the cook, so she can decide."

"Yes, let's have some stew and buns," agreed Jessie.

"I'm sure you will like the stew," said Mrs. Nelson. "I put it up in glass jars. You'll need a quart."

When Benny saw the onions and tiny carrots, he said, "I think we need two quarts, Jessie."

"Yes, maybe we do. The Aldens are all good eaters. We are going to make a fire tonight in the fireplace, and we'll heat the stew on our oil-stove."

"Do you have plenty of wood for the fireplace?" asked Mr. Nelson. "When we were there the last time, we left quite a big pile."

"Yes, we are grateful for it," said Henry. "When we do go home for good, we will leave some, too."

"It's a good cabin," said Barbara. "We like it so much. Now, don't you want a bag for these glass jars?"

"No, we have our knapsacks," said Violet. "Oh, there's the sunflower seed! We want a bag of that, too. And look at the big red apples, Jessie!"

Jessie said, "Apples are good for dessert. They don't have to be cooked. We'll take a dozen."

"What a load you have," said Mr. Nelson.

"Well, there are four of us," said Henry.

"Please don't go, Benny," said Puggsy.

"I'm sorry. We have to go," said Benny. "We have to make a bird feeder."

Mrs. Nelson put her hand gently on her little boy's head. She said, "Don't tease them. They have a long walk back to the cabin. Now, I have put the buns in this little basket with a handle. You don't need to bring it back. I have several. The heavy things will hurt the soft buns."

"You are so kind, Mrs. Nelson," said Jessie. "We'll come again soon."

When the Aldens were out of sight of the store, Benny said suddenly, "Let's stop here a minute and talk. The only thing I can think of is Mrs. Nelson stopping Puggsy when he said, 'We look and look.'"

Henry nodded. "Right, Ben. There is some mystery here, I'm sure of it."

"Me, too," said Jessie. "It is strange, isn't it? They are such friendly people. But I am sure they are hiding something."

Violet said, "I think so, too."

"Well," said Benny, "if you all agree with me that something is wrong, we can go along to our cabin. Then we'll have lots of time to talk. We have two and a half miles to walk."

It was rather late when they reached the cabin.

"It seems to take longer to get home," said Benny.

"It does seem like home," Violet said, going in.

Jessie said, "We always feel at home in our new places, don't we? Just think of the many places where we have lived! And we enjoyed them all."

"That's because we were all together," said Benny. "Let's have supper."

"Oh, Benny! But I guess you're right," said Jessie. "We haven't many dishes. I'll have to find something for the bird feeder."

"No," said Benny. "Take the little basket with the handle. Hang it on the tree."

"Of course!" replied Jessie. She filled it with the sunflower seed. Henry and Benny walked way around the house, because there was no back door. They hung the basket on a low branch of the tree where everyone could see it from the window.

Jessie and Violet were bending over looking at their cooking dishes. "Here's a tin saucepan for the stew," said Jessie. "But it's the only one. There is no other cooking dish but the frying pan."

Violet found one blue bowl, one large white cup, one vegetable dish, and one soup plate.

"That's fine, Violet," said Jessie, laughing. "It's more fun. We each have a dish of some kind, anyway. We'll give Benny the big vegetable dish and I'll take the cup. But I'll fill mine twice."

Henry sat in a chair and rubbed the red apples until they shone. "We'll have to hurry with supper," he said. "It's getting dark."

"We've got lanterns, Henry," said Benny.

"After supper we'll build a fire in the fireplace," said Henry. "Then we can sit around the fire and talk, and the fire will keep us warm all night."

They sat down at the table and Jessie put a different dish before each one. Near the middle of the table were a dozen buns.

The stew was delicious. The Aldens talked while they ate.

"Look what's on our bird feeder," said Benny. It was a big gray squirrel.

"Oh, dear!" said Jessie. "I have heard that squirrels scare away birds."

Violet said, "I have heard that squirrels are simply terrible if they get into a house. We'll have to be careful to keep the door shut."

Henry banged on the window, but the squirrel just sat and looked at him.

"He's clever, though," said Benny. "See him sit still, just as if he's frozen. He doesn't move at all."

Soon the supper was all gone. Only the apples were left. Henry started to build a fire in the fireplace. He used some pine cones, then some small wood, and last of all, two big sticks on top. The fire burned well at once with a fine blaze.

"Now, let's talk about the Nelsons," Henry said. "I think they come here often to hunt for something."

"That's what I think," said Benny. "That's what Puggsy said. Only he said 'look' instead of 'hunt.' It means the same to me."

Jessie said, "And his mother tried to stop him. That's really why we noticed it so much."

The Aldens talked and talked as they ate the red apples. When it was really dark outside, Henry put a fire screen up in front of the fire, and they all crawled into their sleeping bags, which were spread on their bunks.

"Nice and warm, Henry?" asked Benny. "I'm asleep already."

Henry didn't answer. He was already asleep.

They all slept soundly for a few hours. Then one by one they woke up. There was a funny scratching noise on the roof over their heads. Watch began to bark. Then something ran overhead. Watch ran around wildly, barking and barking.

Benny said, "Now, what's that?"

Henry called out, "Jessie! Violet! Are you girls all right? Don't be afraid!"

"What's the matter?" called Jessie.

"I don't know yet," said Henry. "But we'll find out."

CHAPTER 4

Attic Guests

The Aldens got up. It was cold and dark. Not much light came in from the window, and the fire in the fireplace was almost gone.

Henry looked up at the ceiling. He listened. "That must be a squirrel," he said.

"One squirrel?" asked Benny. "It sounds like a dozen!"

"Oh, dear," said Jessie. "I've been told the only way to get rid of squirrels when they get in a house is to kill them."

"We won't do that," said Violet quickly.

"Don't worry, we won't do that," Henry

said. "But maybe we can scare them away. Watch, you lie down! Bring me one of those shovels, Ben."

Benny was nearest the fireplace. He gave a long-handled shovel to his older brother. Henry began to pound on the ceiling with the long handle.

The noise stopped. Not a sound. After a minute it began again. Watch barked and ran around the rooms. Henry pounded again. The noise stopped.

"Now we're in a fine fix!" Henry said. "We can stop the noise, but I don't want to stand here all night pounding with a shovel."

Jessie said, "I guess we'll have to try to sleep and let the squirrels play."

But Henry still stood looking up at the ceiling in the boys' bedroom. It was made of wide boards and was not plastered.

"Ben, come here," Henry called. "There's something funny. The bedrooms have wooden ceilings. But the main room hasn't any ceiling at all. It's open to the roof—look, you can see the beams."

Benny looked up. The squirrels were still running around. He said, "I think when the cabin was new the bedrooms didn't have any ceilings. Someone must have had them put in later to make the bedrooms warmer."

"That attic space over the bedrooms is all closed in," Henry said. "I can't see any trapdoor or any way to get up there from this part of the cabin. The squirrels must get in through some hole in the roof."

"They have a fine little home up there, that's for sure," said Benny.

"Tomorrow I'll go up on the roof and see how it looks," Henry replied. "Maybe we can scare them out and close the hole. Do you think you can sleep, anybody?"

"I can if Watch doesn't keep barking," said Jessie. "We know what it is now, so we're not scared."

Watch stood wagging his tail and looked up at Jessie. She said, "It's all right. You can stop barking."

It was a strange thing. Watch did stop barking. The squirrels scratched and scratched, but

Watch didn't make a sound. Soon they were all asleep, Watch, squirrels, and all.

In the morning the Aldens dressed, and Henry built up the fire before they ate breakfast.

"We'd better go back to the store today and get some advice about squirrels," said Jessie. "Mr. Nelson must know there are squirrels up in that attic. If he has been here three times, he must have heard them."

The Aldens got ready as fast as they could. They took their knapsacks. Henry locked the door and put the key in his pocket.

Benny said, "Farewell, you squirrels! Come again never!"

It was a perfect day. It was even more beautiful than the day before. There was not a cloud in the sky. Jessie said, "I don't think this weather is going to last very long. Grandfather would call this a weather breeder. It means a storm."

"It doesn't look like a storm," said Benny.

"No, Benny, that is what a weather breeder is. A beautiful day that doesn't last. Oh, well, never mind! We can get along even if it rains all the rest of the time."

Halfway to the store, Henry stopped suddenly. He grabbed Watch by the collar and
pointed with his finger. Everyone looked where
he was pointing. It was a deer!

The beautiful animal stood perfectly still.
With soft brown eyes, he looked at the strangers. Then Watch gave a bark, and the deer gave
a high jump. There was a pile of rocks in front
of him, and he went right over them and disappeared.

"What a jumper!" said Jessie. "He must have
jumped ten feet. And it was uphill, too. Oh,
look, there goes another! Look at that jump!"

"That was the doe," said Henry. "Her horns
aren't as big."

"But she can jump as well as the other one," said Benny.

At last they reached the store. They told Mr. Nelson all about the squirrels.

"Yes," he said, "I have heard them. Some people might try to poison them. But that wouldn't work. More squirrels would come. I think your idea of stopping up the hole in the roof is best. Make sure the squirrels are all out, though, before you stop up the hole."

Mrs. Nelson said, "Tom could let you take some boards and a hammer and nails, couldn't you, Tom?"

"Sure," said Mr. Nelson.

Then Jessie told Mrs. Nelson what they wanted to buy. "We want some hamburger and hot dogs for our Benny here, and we want some peanut butter—"

"I wish I could go too," said Puggsy. "Can't I go, Mommy?"

"No, you can't." Mrs. Nelson shook her head. But she was turning red again, and well she might. For Puggsy went on, "If you let me go, I won't hunt for anything."

Tom Nelson laughed, but he was uneasy. He said, "I must tell you that my grandfather built that cabin years ago. I suppose Puggsy thinks it is his cabin."

"I'm sure he does," said Jessie. "It's all right. Don't worry about him. He could come with us, but he would have to stay overnight."

"Do you know where the spring water in the cabin comes from?" Henry asked Mr. Nelson.

"Yes, the water runs downhill from the spring. I know it is close to the cabin. You could look for it. I think there's an old sign."

"Well, here we go," said Jessie. "Got everything, Henry?"

"Yes, some good boards and a hammer and nails."

"We'll be down again soon," said Henry as he went out of the store.

When the store was out of sight, Jessie said, "Isn't that the strangest thing?"

Benny said, "Something is wrong with those Nelsons! They are nice people, too. What's wrong with them, Henry?"

"I wish I knew," answered Henry. "I like

Tom Nelson. But he certainly is worried about something."

"One sure thing," said Benny, "if they want to hide anything, they'd better not take Puggsy along!"

Everyone laughed.

Jessie exclaimed, "Oh, where's Watch?"

They all looked around, but the dog was not there.

"Watch!" shouted Henry as loud as he could. They listened. Not a sound. Henry put down the hammer and nails and boards he was carrying.

"He can't be far away," said Jessie. "Watch!" she called. Then they all heard a faint whine. Instantly they ran toward the sound.

"I can hear Watch, but I can't see him," Benny called.

Henry ran toward some bushes. "Easy, old boy, I'm coming," he called when Watch whined.

Then Henry stopped and pushed the bushes away. Now he saw why Watch had not come.

"It's a hunter's trap!" shouted Henry.

"Watch has caught his hind paw in a trap."

Watch lay on the ground trying to lick his hind paw. When he saw Jessie he looked up and wagged his short tail.

"Hold his foot, Jessie," Henry said, "and I'll force the trap open." He picked up a heavy stick to push the jaws of the trap open.

In less than a minute Watch was free. He held up his back paw and hopped on three legs.

But Henry was angry. He said, "Those steel traps are against the law! Somebody is trying to catch a fox, but he's lost his fox and his trap."

Henry picked up the trap and took it with him. He did not want to say anything to worry Jessie and Violet, but he did not like the idea of someone setting traps in the woods. He hoped it was not anyone who used the hunters' cabin. Indeed, he hoped that there were no strangers at all in the woods. But someone had set a trap.

Jessie looked at Watch's paw, but it was not badly hurt.

They went back to the path, and Benny said, "Henry, I haven't seen you mad for a long time."

"Well, I don't like this," Henry said. "I wonder if the Nelsons know there is a trapper around here." He went back to get the nails and hammer and boards.

The family went on without talking. Then when they were almost at the cabin Benny saw something near the path. It looked like an old, broken sign. He saw an arrow and the word "Spring."

"Look!" said Benny. "Funny thing we didn't see this sign before. We have been past it three times."

Henry stopped. "I guess we were always thinking about something else. I'd like to find that spring. We are almost home, and it won't take long."

Everyone agreed—all but Watch. He was surprised to see his family go back up the hill. He thought he was going home to lunch. But he turned around, too, and trotted along beside Jessie. He did not even hold up his paw now.

There was a path, but it was a poor one. Henry and Benny were both thinking the same thing, but they did not know it. They were wondering if the spring had anything to do with what the Nelsons wanted to find.

"Not many people come to look at the spring, I guess," said Violet. "It isn't very easy walking."

There was something about it that Violet did not like. Maybe it just seemed too lonely.

"I see it," said Benny. "See that wooden cover? The spring must be under it."

The cover was about a yard square. Henry and Benny lifted it from the front edge.

"Good," said Henry. "It stands up by itself."

The Aldens bent over to look inside. The sides of the spring were made of flat stones. The water was clear and about two feet deep.

It was just a spring. There was no mystery about it.

"This never freezes," said Henry.

"Why not?" asked Benny. "How do you know?"

"Watch it, Ben," said Henry. "See, the water is running in and out all the time? Probably the water comes from a spring ten feet deep."

The Aldens turned to go home, and at that

moment it suddenly began to rain. They all ran.

"These boards are getting wet already!" Henry called as he ran.

"You can't fix the roof today," called Benny.

"I never thought it would rain," said Violet.

"It's that old weather breeder," said Benny. "Hurry up, Henry, and unlock the door. My hair is all wet."

When the Aldens were safely in the cabin, Henry put more wood on the fire. Soon the place was warm and cozy. They sat around the fire, cooking hot dogs on sticks.

"Hold my stick," Benny said to Violet. "I'll get my radio. Maybe we can hear a weather report."

The hot dogs were roasted when Benny said, "Listen, here's the report."

"Rain tonight and clearing tomorrow," a voice on the radio said. "Mild weather will continue."

"We aren't going to be like Noah in the ark with forty days and forty nights of rain," said Benny. "One afternoon and night are enough for me."

CHAPTER 5

Benny's Puzzle

The next morning the sun came out.

"What a beautiful day," said Violet. "It's perfect after that rain."

"This is our day to go nutting," Benny said.

If he had known it, it was their day for something else, too.

"Now what shall we put the nuts in?" Jessie asked, bustling around. "I guess the grocery bags are strong enough."

"Let's go right after breakfast," said Benny. "We haven't any beds to make. Nobody can make a sleeping bag."

"I think the nut trees are about halfway to the store," said Henry.

"Nothing to it," said Benny. "A short walk." He took an empty bag and started ahead with Watch.

Nobody knew how many nuts were left under the leaves. The woods seemed to be full of fat gray squirrels. They chased each other in the trees along the way and scolded the Aldens for walking in their woods.

After a while the Aldens found the nut trees. There were a great many of them, close together.

"Here we are," said Jessie. "Let's go to work."

Benny found a long stick and began to turn over the dry leaves. Everyone else got a long stick, too. And there were the hickory nuts! Some had fallen down in their green shells. Some hickory nuts were just lying among the dry leaves, all husked.

"Leave the outside shells on," said Henry. "We have all day to get them off."

The bags began to fill. Nobody had been

there to hunt nuts except the squirrels.

"How many do we want anyway?" asked Benny. "I have fifty-one."

"Why do you ask, Ben? Don't you like to pick them up?" asked Jessie.

"Oh, it's all right," said Benny. "But I am thinking we ought to go on to the store."

"Yes," said Henry. "Let's leave the bags of nuts here."

"No, sir!" said Benny. "I don't trust those squirrels. They would find them just as soon as we went away, and they could open the bags, too. They might eat the bags and all!"

Benny stood still looking at a tree stump. He said, "Henry, we don't want to carry four big bags of nuts a mile and a quarter and then back again. Why couldn't we put the bags in that hollow stump and cover it with heavy branches?"

"We could," said Henry. "Let's try it."

The Aldens put the four bags into the stump and dragged up old branches of evergreen to cover it.

Jessie said, "There! No squirrels can get in

now, Henry."

Henry said, "No, I don't think they can. We'll soon be back anyway. Let's go."

"Well, hello, Aldens!" said Tom Nelson when they pushed the door of the store open.

"Hello," said Jessie, smiling. "It is such a beautiful day after the rain that we went nutting. We picked up four bags of hickory nuts."

"Good," said Tom Nelson. "I know what you can do. Chop up the nutmeats and mix them with chopped apples to make a salad. It's delicious."

Just then Mrs. Nelson and Puggsy came down the stairs. "I heard what you said about the weather," said Barbara, "but I don't think it's going to last. I feel a real storm coming."

"Well," said Benny, "we've seen storms before. Once we were on a trip, and we had a rainstorm and we had to live on potatoes. Nothing but potatoes."

"That makes me think," said Jessie. "We could buy some baking potatoes and roast them in the fireplace."

She picked out a dozen potatoes. She bought

more buns, currant jelly, sugar, and some eggs. Then they started for home.

Henry looked at his watch and said, "It's almost noon."

"It took a long time to pick up all those nuts," said Benny. "I hope they are still in the stump."

The nuts were there, but two squirrels ran away from the pile of branches as the four Aldens came in sight.

When the family reached the cabin, Jessie said, "Now everyone find a flat stone to pound on and another stone to pound with."

"Just like Indians," said Violet. "Nut cracking stones."

They found stones and brushed off the dirt and leaves from them.

Jessie said, "Let's crack the shells now, and later we can pick out the nutmeats."

"No," said Benny. "Let's have lunch first. Peanut butter and jelly sandwiches and milk won't take long."

After lunch they all sat down on the floor, each one before a flat stone. As soon as the nuts were cracked they threw them, shells and all, into the saucepan.

They worked for about an hour, and then Jessie said, "Now let's sweep up this floor. It's just covered with nutshells." She got to her feet and looked around for a broom.

"I looked yesterday for a broom," said Violet. "We haven't got one."

Jessie said, "It seems as if there must be a broom here someplace. But there's not one in sight."

"It seems odd," said Benny. "There ought to be a broom closet right at the end of the fireplace. I remember seeing a cabin built that way."

"Well, there isn't, Benny," said his older sister. "So just let it go."

But Benny began to look for a broom closet. He put the two shovels and the ax in another corner. The fireplace stood out into the room about a foot. Benny looked at this wall. It was made of narrow boards with a line like a crack between each board.

"Here's where the doorknob ought to be," said Benny. "But there's only a little hole." Then he thought what he had said. "A hole! A hole!"

He pulled his knife out of his pocket and opened the biggest blade.

The others came over to watch Benny. In great excitement Benny began to pry at the boards to see if he could find one that would open. And he did! First the top opened, and then he could pull the rest of the door with his fingers.

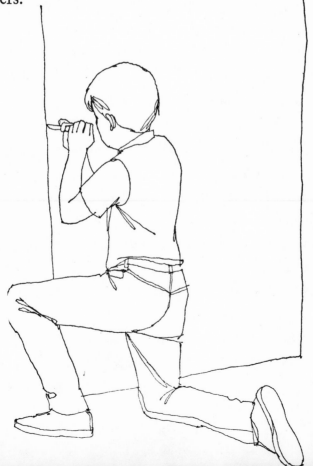

"Well!" said Henry. "Good for you, Ben! That's a real broom closet!"

Jessie exclaimed, "It goes way down to the floor!"

"And there's a broom in it," said Violet.

There was a broom, a brush, a dustpan, and a shelf with cleaning cloths and two bars of soap. Also on the shelf was a little white doorknob with the point broken off.

Henry looked at the closet and the shelf. "This wood is old," he said. "Tom Nelson's grandfather must have built it a long time ago."

"How can you tell it's so old, Henry?"

"Well, put your hand under that shelf," said Henry. "You can feel the marks of the hatchet used to cut the wood. It would be smooth if it were modern."

Benny felt under the shelf. He could feel the chip marks of the hatchet. "That's a neat way to tell," he said. Then Benny ran his hand over the door.

"That's different," said Henry. "The door is planed on both sides, so it is smoother. But it is old, too."

"It's marked, too!" shouted Benny. "Look, Henry! It's not very plain, but I can read it!"

This is what he read:

1M	¼B	¼S	1S	1Y
¼W	1E	?	3F	R

400:15

They all looked at each other. "And what in the world does that mean?" said Jessie. "Copy it, Henry, on a paper, and we can study it."

Henry began to copy the letters, but he said, "It doesn't mean a thing to me. It won't do me any good to study it."

"Me, either," said Benny. "What do you suppose that code means?"

Jessie sat down at the table. "Let's think about it," she said. "We know one thing. And that is that the Nelsons are hunting for something in this cabin."

Benny said quickly, "And it's something they don't want us to know."

Henry looked at his brother. "Right, Ben. They turn red when Puggsy tells us anything. They seem to be ashamed of something."

Violet added, "And they are so nice!"

Jessie nodded. "That's the trouble. But I suppose Tom could have done something wrong a long time ago."

"But what is he looking for?" asked Benny. "Maybe he has been looking for those funny letters. Maybe they tell him how to find some money or something important."

Violet said, "Well, it's strange the Nelsons didn't find them. They must know there should be a broom closet there to keep a broom in."

Henry nodded. "I know what Benny means. I'm sure Tom's father or grandfather cut those letters. They weren't cut for nothing. But the Nelsons don't want to tell us. So let's not say anything about the letters until they do."

"Right," said Benny. "The next time we go down to the store we'll see what they say."

"The afternoons are short in the fall," Henry said. "It's too late to go up on the roof. Put on your radio, Ben, and let's hear what the weather will be."

They waited until the half hour for the weather report.

The announcer said, "A storm is coming from the south and west, but it is not supposed to hit this area. It will go further north and miss us entirely. The northern New England states should prepare for a storm."

"No need to worry then," said Benny. He turned off the radio.

At suppertime it was almost too dark to see.

"What are we going to do tomorrow?" asked Benny as he finished his hamburger.

"Fix the roof," said Henry. "You can help me, Ben. We'll find the hole the squirrels use for a door and nail a board over it."

But Henry didn't know that his plans would be changed for him.

As Benny went to bed, he said, "Maybe that code we found is a secret way to get rid of squirrels." And he laughed.

CHAPTER 6

Snow!

The next day the weather had changed. The sky was very gray. There was no sun. But the Aldens started out for the store.

"It's much colder today," Violet said. She put up her hood and tied it under her chin.

Jessie said, "No blue sky today. Maybe yesterday was a weather breeder, after all. You remember Barbara said she thought a storm was coming."

"Well, never mind," said Benny. "After all, it's too early for snow. And the radio report said the storm would not hit us."

Benny trotted along with Watch. They walked faster this time. They did not stop to look at anything on the path.

"Two and a half miles is a long way on a chilly day," said Jessie, "but it's just a nice walk in good weather. We'd better not stay very long at the store, Henry."

"Right," agreed Henry. He looked up at the sky again. "The clouds seem to be getting heavier," he said. "I hope we can fix that roof before it rains again."

At last the four Aldens reached the Nelsons' store. This time there were a few other customers in the store. They were getting big bags of groceries.

A woman smiled at Jessie. She said, "We think we'll have rain soon, so I'm buying a lot of things. Maybe you folks ought to do the same. Sometimes it rains here for days."

"Thank you," said Jessie gratefully. "We're getting supplies, too. We have to walk over two miles to get here. Henry, pick up some canned meat and bacon while you are on that side, and some spaghetti and tomato sauce. I'll get more chocolate and hot dogs and hamburgers and dry milk."

"I've got more dog food," called Benny.

The other people went out with their bags. Tom said to Henry, "You see we don't get many customers now. The summer people have gone, and many people have moved away for good. I think I'll have to move if I want to make a living."

"Don't move before we do!" Benny said.

As he spoke, Mrs. Nelson came downstairs. She said, "I think it is going to snow. It feels just like it to me." She frowned. She looked worried.

"Snow!" Benny said. "It's too early for snow."

"Yes, it's too early, but just the same you had better go right back. You don't want to get caught on the trail if snow comes. If you wait here you may."

"That's right, Mrs. Nelson," said Henry. "Put up your hoods, everybody, and tie your scarves on tight."

Mrs. Nelson took a quick step toward the girls. She said, "Oh, Jessie, you know I want you to stay, don't you? I don't want you to hurry away!"

"Oh, Barbara, we do," answered Jessie. "Of course we know it. But we mustn't get caught in the storm. Now here we go. Got everything?"

Watch was on his way as soon as the door was opened. The Aldens wasted no time. They walked along the path as fast as they could. Soon they were out of sight of the store.

"Not too fast, Ben," called Henry. "Save your fast walking for the end, like a race."

Benny slowed down. He began to think of the secret code and of Tom Nelson moving away. "Is Tom Nelson running away?" he wondered. Then suddenly he turned around. "What do you know, Henry. It's snowing!" he said.

"It is!" Jessie said. "Maybe it will stop as suddenly as it began."

But it did not. It snowed harder. The snowflakes were small and fine. Even through the thick trees the snow fell faster and faster.

"I wouldn't like to be stuck in the snow!" exclaimed Benny. "Nobody would know where we are!"

"We won't get stuck, Ben," Henry told him. "Don't worry about that. You couldn't really get stuck in the deep snow because we can walk two miles before the snow can get that deep. Just keep going."

Watch was the one who trotted along steadily, without hurrying. He never looked to the right or to the left, just straight ahead.

"Good boy," said Benny. Watch didn't even turn his ears.

"I'd never believe this," said Henry, "if I didn't see it. The snow is already an inch deep."

Jessie added, "Remember, Henry, this is in the woods, too. It must be deeper than this

where there are no trees. Oh, I'm just about frozen. Isn't it cold?"

"Well, we have enough stuff to eat when we
get to the cabin," said Benny. "If we ever get
there. We can make our food last a long time if
we get snowed in."

Uphill and downhill they went, bowing their
heads in the driving snow. The flakes were bigger and bigger. The children could hardly see
the path. They slipped a few times, but nobody
fell.

Watch's legs seemed to grow shorter and
shorter. He could not trot now, he had to hop
along over the deep snow.

But they made it. When Henry unlocked the
cabin door the snow was four inches deep on the
step. They stamped their feet and went in and
locked the door behind them.

"Well!" said Jessie.

Nobody else said a word. They all took off
their jackets and hung them on nails to dry.
Henry fixed the fire, saying nothing. It was already twelve o'clock. Jessie got a pan of water
from the faucet and put it on the stove to heat.

She thought her family needed some hot chocolate. They thought so, too, when they smelled it.

Violet got out the frying pan and soon bacon was frying. When they sat down to eat, Henry said, "Now I have something to say. This is a very early snow. Nobody expected it. It can't possibly last long and we are in no danger."

Jessie said, "Just one thing bothers me. Grandfather must be worrying about us, and the Nelsons probably are, too."

"But we can't do a thing about it," said Henry. "We can't get down to the road and we can't send a message."

"So let's enjoy it!" finished Benny.

"That's exactly what I mean," said Henry, smiling at his brother. "I'm going out in the snow soon to shovel the steps and a narrow path around the house. Then I'm going to clear a small place in the back of the house under the window where the trees were cut down. Right under the bird feeder."

"I'll help you," said Benny. "There are two shovels."

"Thanks, Ben."

It was cold and still snowing hard. The two boys managed to shovel an open square under the window. They threw the snow to one side.

Henry said, "This cleared place will fill up right away, but we can shovel it out again."

"It will be easier the second time," Benny said. "Not so deep."

Henry looked up at the roof to see the squirrels' hole, but he could hardly see the roof! It was deep with white snow. He said, "I guess the squirrels won't have to worry for a while. I'm not going up on the roof today, hole or no hole."

"Another noisy night, then," said Benny. "We could invite the squirrels down and play with them, if we didn't have Watch."

"Now, Ben, don't get any ideas," said his big brother. "I'd just like to know how big that hole is."

The hole was simply enormous. But the Aldens did not know that yet.

CHAPTER 7

Making Do

That night when the Aldens went to bed it was still snowing. And it was getting colder. More than that, the wind was beginning to blow.

"I call this a blizzard," said Henry. "I've never seen anything like it."

And indeed there had never been anything like it in this part of the country at this time of the year. The wind made so much noise that the children did not mind the squirrels at all. They somehow managed to sleep.

But when the family woke in the morning they could hardly see outdoors! The snow was so deep that it covered the lower half of the one window.

"Poor Grandfather," said Violet as she tried to look out. "I'm sure he is worrying about us." She climbed on the window seat and looked over the snow, then she called, "Henry, you won't believe it! The snow is up to the bird feeder and the basket is buried in snow."

Benny, Jessie, and Henry climbed up to look. They could see only the handle of the basket.

"My radio!" shouted Benny. He almost fell off the window seat. "I'll tune in Greenfield and get the news. Maybe they're sending out special messages because of the storm."

Jessie began to get breakfast. Henry started to put on his warmest clothes, but he did not explain why.

"Listen, here's the news," Benny said.

The newsman on the radio said, "As a service to our listeners during the blizzard we are broadcasting special messages. Please listen carefully. Mr. Allan Moore is safe, but he wants his family to know that he can't get home today. The Police Chief wants people to stay calm. The streets will be cleared as soon as possible. The Fire Department wants everyone to be careful about overheating stoves and causing fires. Mr. James Alden wants to notify his grandchildren that they should stay in the hunters' cabin. He will get help to them as soon as he can."

Benny said, "Just like Grandfather!"

"Isn't it?" said Jessie. She was feeling better now, after hearing the news from her grandfather. "I think I shall make some more hot chocolate for breakfast. We all need something hot."

But when she turned the faucet, nothing happened.

"No water, Henry!" she cried.

"I bet the pipe is frozen," said Henry.

"Never mind, never mind!" said Jessie, smiling.

"What's the idea, Jessie?" asked Benny.

"I'm going to make hot chocolate just the same. I'm going to melt some snow."

Henry opened the door wide enough to scoop up the snow with the big saucepan. "Heap it high, Henry," Jessie said. "It will soon melt down."

She put the pan on the stove. The great pile of soft, white snow began to get smaller and smaller. In a little while the water boiled.

"I'll use the powdered milk in the chocolate," said Jessie.

The family enjoyed breakfast. The hot chocolate helped them all.

Then they knew why Henry had put on heavy clothes. He said, "I'm going out, Ben, to see if I can shovel out this new snow around the house. And I want to get the snow cleared again from the bird feeder. Want to come?"

"Of course," said Benny. "Wait till I get dressed."

The snow was up to Benny's waist. The boys dug out the narrow path around the house, throwing the snow off to one side. The wind blew and the snow got in their eyes.

Inside the cabin the girls could hear the two shovels going. "Let's get dressed," said Violet.

Then Jessie said, "Look at that window!"

The snow was disappearing! The girls could see a shovel come in and go out, taking a pile of snow with it.

"Good. We can begin to see out," nodded Jessie. "Those boys are strong."

Soon the Aldens could see each other through the window, two girls on one side and two boys on the other. They waved and laughed.

The boys were tired when they came in to lunch. But Henry said, "After lunch I must go and get more wood. Want to come, Ben?"

"You bet I want to come," answered Benny. "But this time I'm going to wear snowshoes. I don't like to sink down into the snow. It's too deep."

"What are you going to use for snowshoes?" asked Jessie.

"Those two big kettle covers on the shelf. They don't go with any kettles we have here."

"I suppose a long time ago the hunters had two big kettles up here," said Jessie. "I don't know why, though."

"Probably for deer meat stew," said Benny. "I'm glad we don't have to eat that." He could hardly wait to make his snowshoes.

"How are you going to make those covers stay on your feet, Ben?" asked Violet.

"Well, I'm going to use two belts," said Benny. "And I'm going to make two holes in each cover."

Even Henry watched Benny as he punched two long slits in each cover with his biggest knife blade. He used Tom Nelson's hammer to pound with. He slipped a leather belt through the slits in each cover. Putting a boot on each cover, he buckled the straps, using new holes in the belts. He pulled the belts tight and pushed the ends under his boot lacings.

"Good for you, Ben!" said Henry. "Let's see you walk."

What a noise Benny made! Clank, clank!

He said, "This is worse than the noise the squirrels make. But these snowshoes will be fine on the deep snow. No noise at all."

Jessie helped Benny into his sweater and jacket and heavy gloves. He took one shovel to use as a ski pole, and Henry took the ax. Before they went, they shoveled the steps again. Snowflakes were still falling fast. They were whirling around in the wind.

"Those snowshoes really work, Violet," said Jessie, as they watched the boys. Benny was walking on top of the snow, and Henry was wading in up to his waist. "I hope they won't get lost."

"They won't," said Violet. "They'll stay together."

"Now, how can we surprise the boys?" Jessie began to think. She said, "I wonder what Grandfather meant when he said he would send help? Today? Tomorrow?"

Violet said, "I think he meant to go ahead and eat what we have. I hope so."

"That's what I thought he meant," said Jessie. "Let's have sandwiches for lunch. And why don't we surprise the boys with a big chicken stew for tonight? We have a whole chicken in a can, and we can put in a can of spaghetti. We know how to get hot water when we haven't any water."

The girls started to take the chicken meat off the bones. Then they put the chicken and spaghetti with some hot water in the saucepan. Violet said in great excitement, "I've thought of a second surprise for the boys! Snow ice cream!"

"Wonderful!" said Jessie. "We've got plenty of snow for everything. But I've forgotten how to make it. I think we take a little milk and put in sugar and melt it, and then vanilla—oh, but we haven't any vanilla."

The two girls began to think. Then Jessie said, "We could melt the currant jelly and that would make it taste like currant. Just as good as vanilla."

"It would make it pink ice cream!" said Violet.

No sooner said than done. Jessie began to mix the powdered milk and jelly and sugar. "We won't put in the snow until it is time for dessert.

Look, here come the boys now."

Benny and Henry had armfuls of wood. "That wood looks like Henry's work," said Violet, laughing. "All the sticks are the same length."

Benny came first on his snowshoes. He could walk faster. Henry had to lift his feet high over the snow at every step.

Benny called, "We're going right back. We had to leave a few sticks. But wait till I put my muffler on for a belt!"

"I should think so," said Jessie, trying not to laugh. "Want any help?"

"Yes, I do. Maybe one muffler won't go around me."

"One is enough," said Jessie, "unless it is pinching you."

"No, it doesn't pinch me. And isn't this good wood? It's all old and dry. Henry picked it out."

"Wonderful!" agreed the girls.

The boys started back for the rest of the wood. Watch began to bark.

"No, you can't come, Watch," Benny called. "You'd drown."

But Watch went on barking louder and harder.

"He's barking at squirrels, I guess," said Jessie.

"No, he isn't, Jessie," said Violet. "Listen!"

There was a strange low cry outside. The girls opened the door and looked at the snowy path. The boys were just starting out again.

"Oh!" said Jessie. "It's the two deer we saw in the woods!"

The boys had stopped and were looking at the two animals, half buried in the snow. The deer were trying to get on their feet. They fell and got up again.

The boys turned around and came quietly back to the cabin.

Henry said in a low voice, "We don't want to scare them. They think if they find people, they will find something to eat, too."

CHAPTER 8

To the Rescue

The four Aldens left the door open a crack. The deer were half buried in the snow, and they struggled to stand up.

"They don't want any help," said Benny.

"They don't need any," said Henry. "They are up now."

The two deer shook themselves to get the snow off. Still more snow came down on them. But slowly the two animals came toward the cabin. They sniffed. Their soft brown eyes looked at the door.

The deer went down the path that the boys had dug and found the open space. The Aldens went quietly over to the window and looked out. The gentle animals were tired out. They lay down and licked each other.

Benny said, "Listen, I'm hearing things! I think I'm dreaming! Is someone calling?"

But Benny did hear real voices. He opened the door and took one look. Then he shouted, "Henry, put on your jacket and bring me mine!" Then he jumped down the steps to the path.

Henry took both jackets from the hook and struggled through the snow. The girls looked down the path. Something—or someone—was lying in the snow. A man with a little boy on his shoulder was leaning against a tree.

The Aldens forgot all about the deer.

"It's the Nelsons!" said Jessie. "Oh, dear! I'm afraid Barbara has fallen in the snow. We'll just have to wait. We can't go out!"

"The Nelsons have come to help us," said Violet. "I'm sure of that."

"So am I," said Jessie. "Look! Henry's carrying Barbara. I'll get a sleeping bag and put it in front of the fireplace."

"I'll get it," said Violet. She disappeared. Jessie held the door wide open.

Barbara was talking in a weak voice to Henry. "Oh, I'm so ashamed to give out, Henry! I thought I could make it. But I didn't know how bad it was."

Henry said, "Don't say such things about yourself! I wonder you got here at all. You were kind and brave." He put Mrs. Nelson down on the sleeping bag. Jessie put another bag under her head.

"Oh, I can sit up! I'm sure I can," said Barbara.

"You stay right there, Barbara," advised Jessie, kneeling down beside her. "Later you can sit on the couch."

Watch came over and sat down and never moved.

Benny said, "Mr. Nelson is the one who should sit down. He carried Puggsy most of the way." Benny pushed a chair under Mr. Nelson, who dropped into it and leaned back and shut his eyes.

Puggsy was feeling the best of anyone, but

even he was pretty tired. Benny put him into his own sleeping bag and propped him up against a chair.

"Well, well," said Benny. "You came to help us!"

Mr. Nelson nodded. "We tried to, anyway. We were worried about you when it kept on snowing. We didn't know whether you ever got home or not."

Henry nodded, "We might not have."

"I said I was coming to look for you early this morning, but Barbara said she'd come, too. She would be worrying that I was lost. Of course we had to bring Puggsy."

"I'm so thankful you got here!" Jessie shivered. "You might have been lost in the snow."

"We did fall twice, but we got up," said Tom Nelson.

Jessie had a sudden thought. "Are you hungry?" she asked.

"Am I hungry!" shouted Puggsy. "I haven't had anything to eat for a million years."

Henry laughed. "That sounds like you, Ben," he said.

"Well," said Tom Nelson, "it has been a long time. We started out with a big sack of food for you, but we had to leave it in the snow."

Jessie said, "Violet, I'm sure we can eat that stew now. It's all cooked anyway, and it is nice and hot. Now, take seats at the table. I've found three more dishes for chicken stew."

"Chicken stew?" said Puggsy. "I've never heard of that."

"It's delicious," said Benny.

"Well, if you say so," said Puggsy, looking at him.

They all began to eat the chicken stew. Mr. Nelson said, "How thankful we are to be here!" He drew a long breath.

While the others were eating more stew, Violet and Jessie made the snow ice cream. They mixed the soft, white snow with the milk and sugar and currant jelly. It was a lovely pink color.

"Wouldn't Grandfather laugh at this ice cream!" said Benny. Then he told the Nelsons about the message from Mr. Alden that had come over the Greenfield radio station.

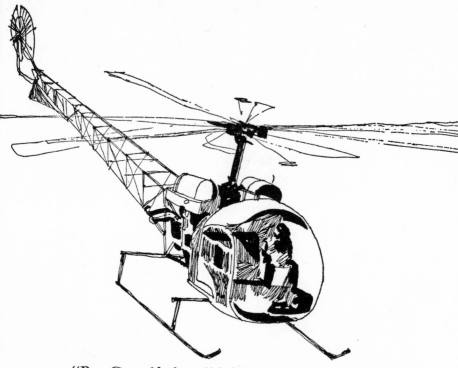

"But Grandfather didn't know that you were coming," he added.

Just then everyone heard a strange humming sound outdoors.

"What's that?" asked Jessie. She stopped to listen.

"A helicopter!" shouted Benny. "I know that sound! Where's my jacket?" He was out of the door in a second, putting on his jacket as he ran. Henry was right behind him.

The sound grew louder. The helicopter seemed to be standing still in the air right above the hunters' cabin.

"The pilot can't land here," Benny said. "What's he going to do?"

"Get back, Benny!" shouted Henry. "The pilot is throwing something out."

Bump! Something hit the cleared spot where the boys had shoveled.

"Hay!" Benny exclaimed. "Just the way they throw hay out to cattle lost in the snow. But how did Grandfather know about the deer? We can't eat hay."

But now Tom Nelson was outside, too. He said, "Benny, it's a haylift. There's something inside the hay. They put the hay around it for a soft landing. It's a good thing you shoveled out this place! That showed the pilot that you can pick up anything he drops."

The helicopter flew low and the pilot waved both arms. The helicopter made such a noise the boys couldn't hear a word. The pilot hovered over the cabin. Suddenly he held a blackboard out of the door.

CAN'T LAND.

MESSAGE IN HAY.

BACK IN 2 HOURS.

The boys nodded their heads back and forth, and waved their arms again.

Off flew the helicopter.

The boys dragged the bale of hay into the narrow path. The others were watching from the window. Then the boys dragged the bale into the house and everyone began to pull off the hay.

"Don't go too near the fire with that hay!" said Jessie. "We don't want a fire as well as a blizzard."

Then they found the packages.

"Canned milk," said Henry. "And canned peaches."

"Loaves of bread," said Jessie.

"And a bag of sugar and lots of hamburger meat," said Benny. "And that's all. It's lucky that the sugar was wrapped in the hay. We would have sugar all over everything if the bag had broken."

"And now where's the message?" asked Henry. "That's most important of all."

"Here it is," said Benny. "A card all done up in plastic."

Henry read it aloud:

From Your Grandfather: The State Police and the Highway Department will get you home as planned. Find something big for a message. Print what you need in large letters. Lay the sign on the snow. The pilot will come again and drop whatever you need. Tell me how you are.

"What can we write our message on?" asked Jessie.

"Oh, dear," said Violet. "We haven't anything big enough! And no paint or ink."

"Let's look around," said Benny. He sat down and began to look at everything in the room. Jessie went into the bedrooms to look. Nothing was big enough. There was not even a big calendar on the wall.

The Nelsons tried to think, too.

"It can be either light or dark," said Violet, "if it is big enough."

"What will you print with?" asked Puggsy.

"Wait until we settle our first problem,

Puggsy," said Henry. "We must find a big card or something."

Benny had looked all around the living room and at last his eyes came back to the window.

"Look!" he said. He pointed to the dark green window shade.

"Oh, Benny," cried Violet. "The very thing! It's the only thing in this whole cabin that's big enough."

Henry stood on the window seat and took down the shade. He unrolled it on the floor.

"You stand on this end, Puggsy," he said. Benny was already standing on the other end. It was perfect for a big sign!

"Now Problem Number Two," said Henry. "We will have to print with something white. And we haven't any chalk. A prize to the one who thinks of something that will work."

"I'd like to get that prize," said Puggsy.

His mother said, "Well, then start thinking, Puggsy."

It was Violet who came up with an idea at last. She said, "I'm not sure it will work. But we can try one letter and see."

"What are you going to print?" asked Barbara Nelson. "What do you need?"

"We need three sleeping bags for you," Jessie said. "You will freeze if we don't get something before night. Now, what's your idea, Violet?"

"I've done this before," said Violet, "but never so big. Print the letters with water first. Then shake on the salt thickly, and when it dries shake off the loose salt."

"I bet it will work," said Benny. "Let's try. Violet, you're the best printer and painter. Start with an *S* as big as this."

He traced a letter about four inches tall for Violet.

"We're lucky to have water," said Benny. He brought a cupful of water. Jessie set down the box of salt.

Violet went down on her hands and knees. She dipped her finger many times in the water and made a big, wet figure 3. Then she shook on plenty of salt. "Let it dry a minute," she said. "I'll go on with the *S* for sleeping bags." Everyone watched her.

After the letter *S* was made, Violet said,

"Now let's shake the salt off the 3."

Henry lifted the corner and shook the salt into the fireplace. A beautiful white figure 3 stayed on the shade!

"Good, good!" shouted Benny. "It works! I knew it would!"

When "3 Sleeping Bags" had been written, Jessie said, "We ought to tell Grandfather why we want them. I think just the word Nelsons would be enough. He'll know they came to help us."

Violet was already printing "3 Nelsons." She said, "I'm going to say 'Fine.' Grandfather will know that we mean we are all fine."

Benny said, "Say thanks for the hay. He will think that is funny."

"Yes, I think he will," said Henry, laughing. "And he'll know it's you, Benny. It sounds like you. It will do him good."

When the sign was done, Henry said, "Let's put it out now. The pilot may come early."

"Maybe we'll have to put stones on the corners," said Benny, putting on his jacket.

"And where will we ever find stones in all this

snow?" asked Tom Nelson.

"Our nut cracking stones!" said Jessie. "Better take four with you. Then you won't have to come back."

There was not much wind now, and it had stopped snowing. The boys laid the big sign on the snow. The wind lifted the corners a little, so they put a flat stone on each corner.

"That's neat," said Benny. Then he stopped short. "Henry," he said, "let's get that hay and put it out here for the deer."

"Good!" said Henry. "They will find it after we go in."

This idea pleased Jessie. She cleaned up the floor. Tom Nelson helped the boys carry the hay out and put it near the bird feeder.

"Listen!" said Benny, turning around again.

"Yes!" said Henry. "The helicopter is coming—lucky we put our sign out right away. The pilot's a little early."

The family inside heard the helicopter, too. They all tried to look out the window at once.

On came the pilot until he hovered right over the boys. They saw him laugh as he read the message. He had his blackboard ready. "Back in One Hour." Then away he went.

The boys rolled up the window shade and took it in. As Benny hung up his jacket he said, "We can brush off the salt later. That shade will be as good as new."

"Let's wash the dishes while we wait," Barbara said.

"Not you," said Jessie. "You just watch."

But Barbara Nelson was already piling up the funny empty dishes.

"Isn't it a good thing we heated water, Jessie?" asked Violet. "It's just right for the dishes."

Tom Nelson felt better now. He had eaten something. He said, "Henry, just where do you think those squirrels are?"

"Come into my bedroom and you'll hear them yourself."

Benny and Puggsy went with them, and right near the chimney they could hear scratchings and scramblings.

"Well," said Tom Nelson, "I should say there was a mama squirrel up there as well as papa.

They must have several children with them. You see the young ones are spring squirrels, and now they are just as big as their parents. I think they plan to live here all winter."

Henry laughed. "And we spoiled their plans. We bother the squirrels instead of their bothering us. They came here first."

"Exactly," said Tom. "They're afraid now. Those squirrels probably have a bushel of nuts up there and a beautiful nest. Goodness knows what it is made of."

Benny said, "I'd like to see that nest. The ceiling is just made of thin boards, isn't it? Couldn't you make a hole in the ceiling, Henry?"

"I could, but I won't," said Henry. "We don't want a family of squirrels coming down to live with us."

Puggsy said, "Dad, do you think the squirrels were down here once?"

"I don't think these squirrels were," Tom Nelson said. He looked around uneasily and went on, "But I think some squirrels got into the big room of the cabin once. We found a newspaper that seemed to have been chewed by squirrels, but no squirrels."

Henry said, "Maybe a hunter shooed those squirrels out and didn't throw away the old newspaper."

"That's what I thought," Tom said, and he still looked troubled. "Squirrels can do a lot of harm to books and papers."

"There's not much they can hurt here," Henry said. Then he remembered that there was something important—something mysterious— the Nelsons wanted to find here. Perhaps it was something squirrels could destroy. Why didn't Tom tell the Aldens what it was? They could show him the code. But he kept his secret.

"We're lucky this cabin has a good roof over us and the squirrels," said Benny. "The snow is four feet thick. It looks just like a big birthday cake that's mostly frosting."

"Four feet!" said Tom. "Yes, it must be. That is a big load for this little roof."

He didn't know that some of that snow was falling through the hole the squirrels had made in the roof. It was piling up in the attic.

CHAPTER 9

Missing Piece

In about an hour the two Alden boys went out to wait for the pilot. They were not a minute too soon, for the pilot was early. Suddenly they heard the roar of the helicopter. It hovered right over them.

The pilot waved to them. First he dropped the bundle of sleeping bags. They were covered with plastic.

"They won't get wet," said Benny. "They landed better than the hay did."

Both boys looked up at the pilot and waved their arms. Up and off went the helicopter.

The boys took in the plastic bundle. Henry found the snaps and took off the plastic cover.

There were two big sleeping bags and one little one.

"How did Grandfather know Puggsy was so small?" asked Benny.

"Well," answered Tom, "I must tell you that Mr. Alden telephoned me before you came to stay in the cabin. He asked me if somebody was always in the store. So of course I told him about my wife and Puggsy. I told him we lived over the store."

"Here's a long box," said Jessie. She opened it and inside she found a small hammer, a box of nails, a box of tacks, two coils of wire, one heavy and one thin.

There was a message that read, "People snowed in sometimes need tools. Maybe the cabin needs repairs. Hope to see you soon. Love from Grandfather."

Jessie put the box of tools away and said, "You know we have never had time to pick out those nutmeats from the broken shells. Come on, let's have a nut party."

"And invite every nut we know!" said Benny. "Everyone is invited. Bring one of

Grandfather's sharp nails for a nutpick."

Jessie put the cracked nuts on the table. The Aldens and the Nelsons sat around, picking out the nutmeats and throwing away the shells.

As they worked, Henry looked across the table at Jessie. He raised his eyebrows. Jessie understood. She nodded.

Then Henry began. "Tom," he said, "I'm going to tell you something. We know you've been looking for something in this cabin."

"That's right!" said Puggsy.

Tom said slowly, "Yes, that is right."

"Well," said Jessie, "we don't know what it is. And you don't want to tell us. But we have found something."

"Oh, what is it?" cried Barbara in great excitement.

For answer, Jessie looked at Benny. "Show them the broom closet that you found by the fireplace," she said.

"There's no broom closet," said Tom, shaking his head.

"Look here," said Benny, and he opened the closet door with his pocketknife. The Nelsons stared in surprise.

"We found some letters carved on the back of this door," Benny went on. "But they don't mean anything to us."

Tom crossed the room almost in one jump. He took one look at the letters on the door and cried, "Barbara, it's here!" Then his voice died away, and he added sadly, "No, it isn't."

The Aldens were really puzzled now. What could this mean?

Barbara saw how troubled they were. "I'll tell you what it is and then you'll understand. You know that Tom likes to bake more than anything else. His father and grandfather had a wonderful recipe for buns. No one has ever made buns just like them. The recipe was a family secret."

Now Tom Nelson said, "My father used to put one special thing in his buns. It made them different."

"Different from any buns in this world!" said Puggsy.

"Oh!" said Benny. "You know the whole story, Puggsy?"

"Yes, I do. If Daddy could find that one thing he could make buns and be rich!"

"Oh, Puggsy!" his mother said. Then she added, "But we think if Tom could make those good buns he might become famous. . . ."

"I begin to see," Jessie said. "But I still don't know what those letters on the door mean—or why you are disappointed."

"I'll explain," said Tom. "It's the recipe for the buns written in a code. See that first line? It begins 'One cup of milk.' I know all those ingredients. The one thing I don't know is still missing. Do you see that question mark? That's what we're looking for—the whole recipe without any question mark."

"I still don't know what all the letters mean," said Violet.

"I'll explain," said Barbara. "They mean:

1 *cup milk*	¼ *cup water*
¼ *cup butter*	1 *egg*
¼ *teaspoon sugar*	?
1 *teaspoon salt*	3 *cups flour*
1 *yeast cake*	*raisins*

Bake at 400° *for* 15 *minutes.*"

"How simple!" said Violet. "When you know the secret."

"They are easy buns, except for one ingredient," Tom said. "But my father never told me what that one thing is. It has always been a family secret. He always put it in himself. He died before he told anyone."

Benny thought a minute. He said, "Why do you think the secret is in this cabin?"

"A good question, Benny," said Tom. "My grandfather built this cabin. And my father used to stay here before the Sportsmen's Club bought it. When my father was dying he said the one word, *cabin*."

"Was the ingredient something like vanilla or brown sugar?" asked Jessie.

"I've tried different things," Tom answered. "But the buns don't taste right. I don't know any more than you do." Then his face brightened and he said, "I know we could make those buns famous!"

Jessie watched his face and he smiled. She loved to see anyone who liked his work so much.

Tom went on, "First I would spend some money to advertise the buns. Then everyone who bought them would advertise them. They are delicious."

"Isn't it too bad that your father didn't tell anybody," said Benny. "If you do find it, be sure to tell somebody. And put a copy of the recipe in the bank, all sealed up."

"Yes, Benny, you're right. I have learned that lesson the hard way," Tom said and looked sad again.

The family began to pick out nuts in earnest now. Soon they were all done. Jessie took the bowl to the kitchen end of the cabin and Henry put the empty shells in the fire.

Jessie broke the nuts with her fingers. Violet chopped the apples with a knife. They mixed the two with salad dressing. Then in the fireplace they cooked the hamburger that Mr. Alden had sent.

Puggsy was tired. "Where do I sleep?" he asked.

Jessie laughed. She said, "The couch makes a double bed for your father and mother. You can sleep in your sleeping bag on the floor right next to the fire."

"You're tough and the bag is soft," said Benny.

Everyone was tired out, even Watch. After the dishes were done, they all went to bed and to sleep. Even the squirrels were quiet.

Henry's and Benny's watches ticked along, but everything else was quiet. At four o'clock in the morning, the wide, loose board in the ceiling of the boys' room began to bend. It squeaked. Watch heard it, but Jessie had told him not to bark at the squirrels any more.

The big board bent some more and it squeaked some more. One end began to hang down. Still Watch did not bark. Slowly the board bent more and more. Then suddenly the other end broke and down crashed the board!

What a noise! The board fell on the floor with a great bang. That was bad enough. But after it came the squirrels' nest, five big fat squirrels, a bushel of nuts, and four feet of soft snow. It was the snow piling up below the hole in the roof that broke the board.

Everyone jumped out of bed, half awake. Now Watch couldn't keep still. The five squirrels ran around wildly with Watch after them. Watch didn't know which one to chase so he chased them all. They scolded and chattered and Watch barked and barked. What a terrific noise!

"What shall we do?" cried Jessie.

"I don't know," said Henry. Everyone stood still, even the Nelsons, just watching the chase.

Benny shouted, "We'll have to catch the squirrels!"

"They will spoil this house," Violet said.

"They are turning it upside down!" shouted Puggsy, but he thought this was as good as a circus. He was having a wonderful time.

The others were not. They were wondering how to catch five squirrels.

"Can't we put them out in the snow?" Jessie asked.

"No, the snow is too deep," said Violet. "They wouldn't have anything to eat. And they haven't any home in the trees."

The animals were not still a minute, and Watch ran about wildly. He chased one squirrel and slid on the floor and found another squirrel running ahead of him.

Henry looked around for something to make a trap. He could not see anything except an old wooden box in one corner. Maybe the hunters had used it to bring in supplies.

Henry shouted, "Let's try to get the squirrels one by one into this box!"

"But how are you going to keep them in it?" asked Jessie. "It hasn't any top. They'll jump right out."

"I was going to turn it upside down over them," Henry said. "But I guess when we try to put the second one in, the first one will crawl out."

"Wire!" shouted Benny. "Grandfather sent us wire and nails with the tools." He ran to get them.

Everybody watched as Benny took the wooden box. He put a row of nails around the top on all four sides. He pounded the nails in just part way.

"I don't see what good that will do," Violet said. "It looks like a puzzle to me."

"Wait," said Benny. He took the roll of wire and began to run it back and forth across the box top. He wound it around the nails as he worked.

Suddenly Jessie understood. "It's just like darning a hole in a sock!" she said. "Now you're going to weave the wire through in the other direction."

"Right!" said Benny. "I'm going to leave a hole at one corner that's big enough for the squirrels to crawl through. See, we'll put the box on its side and put some nuts in it."

Barbara said, "Yes, if we're quiet, maybe the squirrels will go into the box for the nuts."

"Poor Watch," said Jessie. "I'll have to tie

you up. I know it isn't fair to see those squirrels loose while you're tied up, but I have to do it." She put him in the girls' bedroom.

Jessie found some nuts and bread to go into the box. Everything was ready.

Now that there was no dog, the squirrels stopped running. Everything was quiet. The squirrels sat as if they were frozen. Slowly one squirrel moved toward the nuts. He went into the box. The others could hear him eating nuts. Twenty minutes passed, and the last squirrel crawled in. All five of the squirrels were in the box.

Tom set the box right side up and put a board over the hole in the corner.

The Aldens and Nelsons looked at each other and drew a long breath.

"What a strange thing to happen to this family," said Jessie.

"Who would ever have five squirrels in a box at once?" asked Violet.

"Who but the Alden family!" said Barbara Nelson.

"I think we have had enough adventures,"

said Jessie. "I'm glad we're going home soon. Let's have breakfast. It's after five o'clock."

"My, it's cold, isn't it?" said Violet, shivering.

"It's the hole to the attic," said Henry. "Put on your jacket, Violet. I'll do something about the hole after breakfast."

He went to look at the pile of leaves and snow on the floor, but he couldn't get very near. It was the weight of the snow falling through the hole in the roof that had been too much for the ceiling.

The Aldens and Nelsons put on jackets and ate breakfast. Watch growled, and inside the box the squirrels still scolded. They missed their cozy nest.

After breakfast Henry found that the snow on the bedroom floor had melted. He stood on a chair and with Tom's help nailed the board back in place in the bedroom ceiling.

"What a mess," said Jessie. She began to pick up the nuts and put them into a paper bag. Benny helped her.

"Look at all this stuff those squirrels used for their nest," Benny said.

Puggsy ran over to see. Benny pulled out an old ribbon, many dry leaves and sticks, many chewed up pieces of paper, rags, strings, and nutshells.

"See the pretty blue card," Puggsy said. He held up a small piece of heavy blue cardboard. On it was written "Egg Noodles."

"Here's another blue one," the little boy said and handed Benny one that said "Sugar Cookies."

"Somebody's recipes," Benny said. Then something popped into his head. "Puggsy, help me look for more blue cards—quick!"

The two boys looked and looked. Puggsy got tired, but Benny wouldn't give up. He found the torn corner of another blue card. No good. Then hidden by some leaves he saw one more blue card. Turning it over he saw just one word at the top. *Buns.* It was enough!

"Tom! Come here! Come here!" Benny shouted. "Look at this for me—I just saw one word. Is it . . . ?"

Tom took the blue card, then he cried, "A miracle! Barbara! A miracle—look!" He gave the card to his wife and both of them stood there with shining faces.

"Is it—is it the buns, your grandfather's buns?" Benny asked. "Is the whole recipe there, nothing missing?"

"Oh, yes!" Barbara said. "Benny, you found it. The missing ingredient is here!"

"Don't tell me what it is," Benny said quickly. "I don't want to know."

"No," said Barbara. "But one thing is sure, we'll call them Benny's Buns because you found the recipe."

"I'd like that," agreed Benny. He nodded.

Nobody could believe the hunt was over and the recipe was found at last.

Tom was thinking. He said slowly, "Those blue cards remind me of something. When I was a little boy I used to hear Mother tell my dad to use one of his blue-card recipes. I just thought she meant special ones. I didn't know the recipes were really written on blue cards."

"But how did the cards get in the cabin attic?" asked Barbara. "That's still a mystery."

"Yes," agreed Tom. "There isn't any way to

get up in the attic from the main part of the cabin. No trapdoor or anything. Well, the important thing is that you found the card, Benny. And now I can make buns."

"Maybe we can find something else," Benny said. But although he looked carefully, he could not find anything except leaves and twigs.

Jessie said, "I'm walking around in a dream. Nothing seems real."

Puggsy said, "I feel like that when I get up too early."

"Let's rest and then clean up the cabin," Henry suggested. "We want to be ready to go when the men from the Highway Department get here."

It was about noon when the Aldens heard sounds, the scrape of snowshovels and the voices of men. They opened the front door and went out to meet their rescuers.

The box of squirrels stood on the steps, but Watch was quiet now. He seemed to know he was going home.

CHAPTER 10

A Surprise in Store

Three men from the Highway Department and a state policeman reached the cabin. They had shoveled a narrow path up the hill from the road.

"We're glad to see you!" Henry called.

The men waved. They knew there would be seven people and a dog and a lot of luggage. But the box of squirrels was a surprise.

"Well, now!" said one red-faced shoveler. "And why do you want to carry five squirrels home? There's plenty in my backyard you can have."

Jessie explained. "They were in the cabin attic with a bushel of nuts. You see, there is a big hole in the roof. If we let them go, the squirrels will starve."

"Starve? *Squirrels* starve?" repeated the man. "Not them! Just put your bushel of nuts handy on the steps and let 'em go. You'll see! Did you say a hole in the roof? They'll take all the nuts back before night."

All the men nodded, laughing.

"But look at the snow on the roof," said Henry. Just the same though, he put the bag of nuts on the steps. Then he took the board off the squirrel box. In a minute one squirrel came out and looked at the bag. Out the others came, one by one. They sat perfectly still on the steps.

The sergeant said, "Mike knows. Those squirrels will be all right. You could have shooed them out the door any time."

Tom Nelson laughed. "Yes, I believe you," he said.

Mike said, "You see that tree with the big hole? That will make a good nest and those squirrels will find it."

By now the Aldens and Nelsons were dressed to leave.

"Mr. Alden will be glad to see you," said the sergeant. "He's waiting in his car. He said he couldn't stay at home."

The procession started. Two shovelers went first, then the Aldens and Watch, then another shoveler, then the Nelsons, and last the sergeant.

The path was long and slippery. Snow was piled high on both sides. It was like walking in a tunnel. Even Tom could not see over the top. It seemed as if they would never get down to the road.

At last Benny and the others saw the station wagon. Grandfather was sitting in the driver's seat, waving out the window.

What a happy meeting it was! The sergeant watched a moment, then roared away on his motorcycle to help someone else. The workmen waved.

Mr. Alden said, "I feel as if I'll never let you out of my sight again. But I will."

Violet said, "Of course you will. But right now I want to sit beside you in the car."

"Good," said Grandfather. "We can take seven people—eight people and a dog—in this car. I am grateful to you, Mr. and Mrs. Nelson, for coming to help my family. I want you to stay with me until the snow is cleared and you can get home."

"We did have a great adventure, Grandfather," said Benny. "Jessie said we would."

"Oh, so you did have an adventure!"

"Yes," Benny went on. "Henry says it was really a mystery. But it is solved now."

"Tell me about it when we get home," said Mr. Alden as he started the car.

Puggsy said, "We didn't bring the box of squirrels."

"What?" asked Grandfather. "I hope not."

Benny said, "We'll tell him later about the squirrels, Puggsy. It will be good to get home. I'd like some clean clothes and a bath."

"Well, Ben!" said Henry. "That doesn't sound like you. You don't like baths too much."

"Me either," said Puggsy, "but my mother gives them to me just the same."

When the station wagon came up the drive, Mr. and Mrs. McGregor opened the door. They both worked for Mr. Alden.

"We are glad to see you!" Mrs. McGregor said. "And Watch! You come with me, Watch, and see what I have for you."

Henry said to his grandfather, "Something very important has happened to the Nelsons. We must tell you right away."

"Never mind putting your things away just now," said Mr. Alden. "Just sit down and tell me what the mystery was."

Benny told most of the story. But they all helped him. Mr. Alden understood all about the recipe for buns. He knew how valuable it must be. He turned to Tom Nelson and asked him for his story.

Tom could hardly talk fast enough. "It's too good to be true. For years I've wanted to make buns like my grandfather's and now I can."

"You can make a few right in my kitchen," said Mr. Alden, smiling.

"Oh, I'd like that," replied Tom. "I can make them for supper. There will be enough time for them to rise."

Benny said with a nod, "Grandfather, Tom is

a good worker, but business is bad out in the country where his store is. If he can get more money, he may start a store in town."

"I might be able to help," replied Mr. Alden. "But of course I have to try a bun first." His eyes twinkled.

"Where is your kitchen, Mr. Alden?" asked Puggsy.

Grandfather said, "Benny, take Mr. Nelson out and show him the kitchen. Puggsy can go too if he likes."

Tom was delighted. They went to the kitchen at once. Benny explained to Mrs. McGregor all about the buns.

"Fine," said the good lady. "Help yourself, Mr. Nelson. Flour is here, sugar here, eggs—"

"In the refrigerator," said Tom, smiling. "I am used to strange kitchens. I think I can find everything I want. I can even find a bowl." He took down a yellow mixing bowl as he spoke.

Benny asked, "Do you find that strange thing here? I mean that question mark. Do we have any?"

"Yes, I found it," said Tom. He winked at

Benny. "It is very common. Everyone has it. But it is still a secret."

Benny and Puggsy and Mrs. McGregor watched Tom as he mixed the buns and set them to rise. He put the bowl in a warm place with a cloth over the top. Then Tom and the boys went back to the rest of the family.

"I watched Tom," said Benny. "But I never saw him put in anything strange."

"Well, I put it in," said Tom. "You just didn't notice. I'm going to call them Benny's Buns."

The buns rose to the top of the bowl. Tom kneaded them down again. Later, he made them into balls. He put the buns very close together. Then he set them to rise again.

"These are sweet," he said. "They go better with dessert."

"Ice cream for dessert," said Mrs. McGregor with a smile. "We have four different kinds in the freezer."

When the dessert came, everyone was excited. The buns were tall, and light as a feather. A raisin was on the top of each. Everyone watched as Grandfather took a bite.

"Now these are amazing, Mr. Nelson!" he said. "I never ate such delicious buns! And I can't tell what makes them so different, either."

"That's good," said Tom. He was happy. And Barbara was happy to see her husband doing the thing he loved so much.

Next morning Mr. Alden said to Tom, "I'd like to take you down the street to meet some people. You know that shoppers come here from many other towns."

Benny looked at Henry and laughed. They knew their grandfather was up to something.

Before he went, Mr. Alden asked Mrs. McGregor if she needed anything.

"Yes, Mr. Alden. Get some hamburger and hot dogs for Benny. I'll bake some beans in the electric bean pot and put the hot dogs on top."

"Oh, boy!" said Puggsy. "I like that. I wish I could go."

"You may," said Grandfather, looking at Mrs. Nelson. "If your mother is willing. In fact, everyone can go."

They all started off, except for Henry. He had to get ready to go back to college. Watch did not go either, so they had more room in the car.

Grandfather drove past the supermarkets, past the school and many stores. Then he turned around and came back another way.

"I know!" said Benny. "You want to stop at Franklin's Store for the hot dogs."

"Right," said Mr. Alden. "Franklin's has the best meat in town. And the best groceries."

Mr. Alden parked the car in front of the store. The sign said:

Roger Franklin, Meats and Groceries

Mr. Franklin had to laugh when the whole family came in at once. He was busy with other customers, but he said, "Good morning, Mr. Alden. I'll be with you in a minute."

"Don't hurry," said Grandfather. "We'll look around."

Benny whispered to Jessie, "Look at Grandfather's face! Doesn't it look as if he's up to something?"

"I'm sure he is," said Violet. "I noticed it when he asked Mr. Nelson to ride down the street."

But nobody ever knew what Grandfather's plans were until he was ready to tell them.

At last the other people went out, smiling at Puggsy as they passed him. It seemed as if people always smiled at Puggsy.

"Just some hamburger and hot dogs, Roger," said Mr. Alden. "And do you have any sweet buns?"

"No," Roger Franklin shook his head. "I

don't carry baked things. I wish I did. I could sell them all right. Maybe someday—" He did not even finish the sentence.

Grandfather sat down on a stool and whirled around and around. He made them all laugh, he looked so funny. They were all waiting for Mr. Alden to surprise them.

Suddenly he did. He said without a smile, "The store next to you is empty. And there is a door between." He pointed.

"Yes, I'd like to use that store," said Mr. Franklin. "But I can't afford to buy it. I really need more room."

Benny burst out, "If you had that store, you could have a bakery department!"

Mr. Alden didn't even smile then. He was as sober as a judge. He said, "I see my grandson has guessed my plan."

"Your plan?" The storekeeper was puzzled.

"Let me introduce a baker, Mr. Tom Nelson," said Mr. Alden. "He makes buns from a secret recipe. They are called Benny's Buns."

"After Benny, I suppose," nodded Roger Franklin. He began to understand.

Puggsy said, "That's not all he makes. My dad makes pies and birthday cakes and doughnuts and cookies."

"Oh, he does!" said Mr. Franklin. He stared at the little boy.

"Yes, he's the best baker in the world," said Puggsy.

Mr. Franklin looked at Mr. Alden. He said, "That would be a good thing for Franklin's Store, wouldn't it—to have the best baker in the world in my store."

Grandfather said, "I see you are a quick thinker. If you want to rent that corner store, I think Tom might work for you. Perhaps you don't know that I own that empty store."

The two young men looked at each other. Tom liked Roger, and Roger liked Tom.

Tom said, "I think we could make a go of it. This is my wife, Barbara. She helps in our store in the country. And so does Puggsy. He's quite a salesman."

"I should imagine so," said Roger Franklin, laughing.

"Let me show you the empty store," Mr.

Alden said.

He unlocked the door between the stores and they all went in. It was a bright, sunny place with many windows.

"What a perfect place for a bakery," said Violet. "We girls will stop here on the way home from school to buy buns."

Mr. Alden said, "That's fine, my dear. But this place must be cleaned and painted. And this wall must be taken down to make one big store. It will be a while before you can buy buns."

Benny said, "But not *too* long, Grandfather, if you have anything to do with it."

"That's the stuff, Ben," said Puggsy.

CHAPTER 11

One More Question

Benny was right. It did not take too long to fix the store. First, some carpenters took down the wall between the two stores to make one big room.

Benny noticed one special carpenter. He was an old man. He was slow, but he did fine work. He kept looking at Benny and Puggsy with a twinkle in his blue eyes. The Aldens noticed that he listened to every word they said. The old man always stopped pounding for a minute when they talked about the cabin or Tom Nelson's baking.

Jessie said, "I wonder why that old carpenter is so interested? He's a good workman. He fixed all the windows so that they don't rattle."

But when the painters came everyone forgot the old man. They painted the walls bright yellow. Franklin's Store was painted the same color. Now it was one big store.

A gray tiled floor was put in, and the windows were washed until they shone. Big stoves and refrigerators were moved into the bakery side. A new sign was put up outside:

FRANKLIN'S STORE

BENNY'S BUNS

That was not all. The radio carried news about the store and the newspapers had pictures of Tom, Barbara, Puggsy, and Benny.

The Nelsons bought white uniforms. Barrels of flour came rolling in, barrels of sugar, boxes of eggs.

At last the store opened. It was a Saturday. Benny and Puggsy were there, but Henry was at his college.

People were interested in the new store. There was no doubt about that. When the Nelsons and Roger Franklin came to unlock the door early Saturday morning, there were six people waiting on the steps.

Benny and Puggsy put on their white uniforms at once and stood behind the counter. They sold buns with Mrs. Nelson. Puggsy was too young to take the money and make change, but he could sell buns and put them in bags. Everybody smiled when they saw him and the women said, "How cute!"

People who came to Franklin's Store went into the bakery. People who came into the bakery went into the grocery department. Roger Franklin began to sell twice as much because he now had a bakery.

A woman came in and said, "I'm interested in these buns. There must be a story about the secret recipe."

"Yes, there is," said Puggsy.

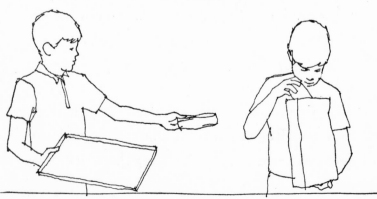

A crowd gathered around Benny and Puggsy. When they told about Watch chasing the squirrels, everyone laughed.

"That's a wonderful story," the woman said. "I like those letters on the closet door. Do you know what the question mark stands for?"

"No," answered Puggsy. He shook his head. "Nobody knows except my dad and my mother."

Just as Benny was getting hungry the door opened and in came Mr. Alden, Jessie, and Violet.

"How are you doing?" asked Mr. Alden.

"Very hungry," said Benny.

Tom laughed. "That's right. But we are selling so much we can't stop to eat."

"That's why we came," said Mr. Alden. "You need a change. We'll sell while you go out to eat lunch."

"We planned to eat buns and coffee right here," said Tom.

"Never mind," said Mr. Alden. "You'll work harder when you come back. Just give me your white uniform. Violet can wear Benny's."

Barbara gave her uniform to Jessie, and soon everyone was ready. His friends thought it was a joke to find Mr. Alden working in a bakery.

The four hungry workers went down the street to a restaurant. On the way people stopped them to say how good Tom's baking was.

While they waited for lunch Benny heard a girl say, "I'm delighted to have a real bakery here. I love that little Puggsy at the counter."

The man with the girl said, "I'd go in just to hear him talk."

Benny and Puggsy made faces at each other.

It was a long day, but a happy one. The Nelsons had dinner with the Aldens before going to their home over the old store.

Puggsy said, "I do miss the squirrels. It was fun to see Watch chase them."

"Well, I don't miss them," Jessie said. "But I do wonder where they went."

Benny said, "Listen, some day let's go back to the cabin and see if we can find the squirrels."

"We could take a lunch with us," Violet said.

Jessie looked at Tom and said, "I still don't know how that blue card got up in the attic over the bedrooms."

Tom answered, "I don't either."

Not long after that on a beautiful day the Aldens and the Nelsons went up to the hunters' cabin. Before they reached the cabin Watch began to bark.

"Listen!" said Benny. "That's pounding!"

They walked faster. A ladder was leaning against the side of the cabin. A man on the roof was pounding shingles. He saw them and waved.

Jessie said, "That's the carpenter who worked on Franklin's Store. Remember?"

Benny shouted, "Did you get all the squirrels out of the attic first?"

"No squirrels there!" called the carpenter. "I looked." Then he pointed at the tall tree in front of the cabin. "I think you'll find your squirrels in that tree. There's a lot of 'em."

"Oho!" Puggsy said. "Mike said they might move into that tree. And there they are."

At first no one could count the squirrels.

They were running around in the tree, chasing each other. At last Benny was sure there were five. Not a nut was left on the step.

Benny said, "I bet they took every nut into that hole before night."

"Well," said Violet, "we don't have to worry about the squirrels. Let's have our picnic lunch in the cabin. It's too cold to eat outdoors."

The carpenter called down, "I'm leaving now. You can have your picnic without any pounding."

"No hurry," answered Jessie. "We'll go in and look around."

"I'd like to talk with you before I go," said the man.

"Now what does he want?" wondered Benny. He took out the key and everyone went into the cabin. Barbara and Jessie began to put the lunch on the table.

In a few minutes the carpenter tapped at the door and Puggsy let him in. He sat down on the couch, holding his old felt hat. He looked at the Nelsons and said, "My name is Don Perry. When I was working in the new store I heard you tell how the blue recipe card was found up here."

Tom Nelson said, "Yes, that was the strangest thing. I'm sure my father wanted me to have that recipe card. But I have never been able to guess how he thought I could find it."

"He never knew a thing about the new ceiling," said the carpenter. "After your father died, the cabin was sold to the Sportsmen's Club. They told me to shut in that part over the bedrooms to make them warmer at night."

"I told you so," said Benny.

The old man went on, "When I was putting up the new ceiling I did notice some old papers on a beam. And there were some blue cards, too. But I didn't think anything about it then."

Jessie said, "We thought the squirrels carried them up there."

"No," said Mr. Perry. "Old Mr. Nelson put them there, and I nailed 'em in."

Tom Nelson said, "This explains everything. I never knew that the attic was closed after my father died. I thought the ceiling had always been there. I'm glad we know."

"Oh, I'm glad we got caught in the snow," exclaimed Jessie. "If it hadn't snowed, we wouldn't have found the recipe. And if the snow hadn't been heavy, the ceiling wouldn't have fallen down."

Violet added, "Now we don't have to worry about anything—the squirrels, the recipe, or Benny's Buns."

Tom Nelson laughed. "The recipe is in the bank and safe in my head."

"And in mine," said Barbara.

"But not in mine," said Puggsy. He shook his head sadly.

"A good thing, too," Benny said. "If you knew that recipe you'd tell everybody. You couldn't help it."

And to this day, Tom and Barbara Nelson are the only ones in the world who know the recipe for Benny's Buns. And they will never tell—until, of course, Puggsy grows up enough to keep a secret.